Troll
SWAP

FOR
eve, tess,
Aurora
& eLsA...

...the
goodest
good little
girls I know

First published in 2013 by Nosy Crow Ltd
The Crow's Nest, 10a Lant Street
London SE1 1QR
www.nosycrow.com

ISBN 978 0 85763 162 6 (HB)
ISBN 978 0 85763 163 3 (PB)

Nosy Crow and associated logos are trademarks
and/or registered trademarks of Nosy Crow Ltd.

Text and illustrations copyright © Leigh Hodgkinson 2013

The right of Leigh Hodgkinson to be identified as the author
and illustrator of this work has been asserted.

A CIP catalogue record for this book is available from the British Library.

Printed in China

1 3 5 7 9 8 6 4 2

Troll
SWAP

nosy
crow

Leigh
HODGKINSON

Say hello to

Timothy Limpet.

Timothy Limpet is a hairy troll
who lives somewhere far away.

Trolls are messy, mucky creatures. Trolls live in damp, dark, squelchy caves. Trolls love scaring the heebie-jeebies out of anyone they can.

Timothy Limpet is **not** like other trolls. Timothy Limpet is **nice** and **polite** and **tidy**. Timothy Limpet's **cave** is not at all damp, dark or squelchy, thank you very much.

The other trolls
think that Timothy Limpet
is a particularly rubbish troll and
not at all **like them.**

Meanwhile . . . somewhere else . . .

Say hello to

Tabitha Lumpit.

Tabitha Lumpit is a little girl
who lives in a house with
her mummy and daddy.

Most little boys and girls are nice.

> Please may I help you?

Most little boys and girls are polite.

> Who would like to share my sweets?

Most little boys and girls are tidy.

> What can I tidy up next?

Tabitha Lumpit is **not** like other little boys and girls.

Tabitha Lumpit is loud and loopy and messy. Tabitha Lumpit has a laugh like a giant foghorn. Tabitha Lumpit would rather pick her nose than a flower any day of the week.

When Tabitha Lumpit sees a muddy puddle . . .

YIPPEE!

. . . she cannot stop herself from jumping in it and making a super-splashy muddy mess.

All Tabitha Lumpit's mummy and daddy want is for her to be nice and polite and tidy, just like them.

Being like most other little boys and girls is almost **impossible**, thinks Tabitha Lumpit.

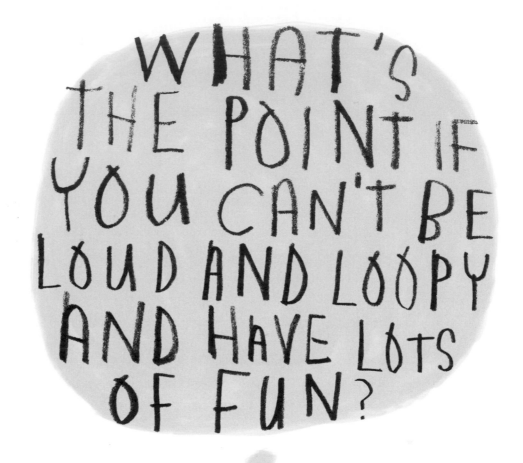

WHAT'S THE POINT IF YOU CAN'T BE LOUD AND LOOPY AND HAVE LOTS OF FUN?

And being a disgusting troll just isn't as **easy** as it looks, thinks Timothy Limpet.

Is it really too much to ask to want a nice quiet life without big burps and bad manners?

But then, something happened that changed **everything**. Tabitha and Timothy were not looking where they were going, when . . .

CLONK!

Tabitha Lumpit said hello to Timothy Limpet.
And Timothy Limpet said hello to Tabitha Lumpit.

HELLO! I AM A GOOD LITTLE GIRL CALLED TABITHA LUMPIT—AND WHO ARE YOU?

hello! I am a big, scary troll called Timothy Limpet.

"YOU DON'T SEEM VERY TROLLISH. YOU SEEM NICE AND POLITE AND TIDY–A BIT LIKE I AM SUPPOSED TO BE,"

said Tabitha.

And you don't seem very good-little-girlish. You seem loud and loopy and messy — why, a bit like I am supposed to be,

said Timothy.

This gave them both a **swappingly** good idea . . . .

. . . so they swapped places! The other trolls were amazed by what a first-class troll Timothy had become.

GO, TIM, GO!

OOOH!

ROAR!

WOWZER!

And Tabitha's mummy and daddy couldn't believe what a nice and polite and tidy little girl Tabitha was.

Good work, Tabitha!

And Tabitha Lumpit's mummy and daddy
soon started to miss the OLD Tabitha.

Now life seemed just a tiny bit dull.

Timothy found that once everything was squeaky clean, he soon got a bit thumb-twiddly.

boring!

Here, everyone was nice and polite and tidy, just like him. Here, he simply wasn't special at all.

And **Tabitha** found that picking her nose, being loud, messy and jumping in squelchy mud didn't surprise anybody. Here, that was just ordinary.

BORING!

They both **knew** that there was only one thing for it . . .

It was time to swap back and
both go home where they

belonged.

And they all lived **happily** . . .

BOING! BOING!

. . . and LOOPILY ever after.